Scowl's Nest

JENNIFER HUDES

SCOWL'S NEST

Cover Design by: Bobbie Zislis and Ed Hanna

FOR LUKA,
WHO WILL ALWAYS BE MY ANIMAL FRIEND.

SCOWL'S NEST

CAST OF CHARACTERS

TESS Owl. Protective, ambitious.

HEDGE Hedgehog. Skeptical, loyal, humorous.

SASHA Pig Fairy. Highly confident.

BARK Talking Tree. Low energy.

SCOWL Spotted Owl. Negative, bitter, tough.

FAIRY EXPRESS EMPLOYEE Robotic voice.

GROUP OF SQUIRRELS Apprehensive.

3 BABY OWLS Cute and bouncy.

CONTENTS

Description

A children's play that tells the story
of a group of animal friends who set
out on a journey to help find a
missing egg. The goal is to help an
owl named Tess find her stolen egg and
make it back before all of her eggs
hatch. To reach their destination,
Tess and her friend Hedge will need to
learn how to trust a Fairy, pass
through dangerous territories, and
outsmart a vengeful Scowl the Owl.

SCOWL'S NEST

ACT ONE

SCENE ONE

SETTING: The forest near TESS'S nest

(Characters in the Scene: SCOWL, BARK, HEDGE, TESS.)

SCOWL

(Puts eggshells near TESS'S nest.)

I built a nest that will not let them roll off again. I'm going to steal one egg and then lay it with the others. These eggshells will make the owl think that the egg fell on its own.

BARK
Why is that owl talking to herself? She doesn't look like the ones I see around here.

1

SCOWL'S NEST

                    HEDGE
I just have to curl up in a ball or dig
a hole with myself in it if it comes
any closer.

    (HEDGE disappears.)

                    BARK
What brings you to these woods? I
rarely see Spotted Owls.

                    SCOWL
Our species isn't doing well. That's
how it's always been. What part of your
tree can I use to scratch my claws?

                    BARK
The top corners. What do they call you?

    (SCOWL scratches her claws.)

                    SCOWL
Scowl. Great wood you have here.

                    BARK
The finest, I've been told. Coming from
you, that's a compliment. You're the
first Spotted Owl to visit my wood.

    (SCOWL   leaves   the   tree   and
disappears.)

Hedge, you can come out now. Scowl is
gone.

SCOWL'S NEST

                    HEDGE
Yes! I won't be an owl's meal today.
I'm gonna say hi to Tess.

    *(TESS is busy getting food for
    herself.)*

                    HEDGE
Tess! Bark just talked to a Spotted
Owl.

                    TESS
Wow. I've only heard about them. I felt
my eggs move again while you'd been
gone.

                    BARK
How are you guys--friends again? I
thought that owls eat hedgehogs?

                    TESS
I only eat specific types of prey like
small mice, not the large rodents or
hedgehogs. Never will I ever eat a
hedgchog.

                    BARK
Hey look out! That Spotted Owl is in
your nest!

    *TESS flies back to her nest, however
    she is struck by the size and weight of
    SCOWL.*

                    HEDGE
Wake up Tess.

SCOWL'S NEST

                    TESS
I feel pain in my everything. A bird
stole my egg.

                    BARK
I saw the owl putting eggshells
everywhere before this happened. I
should have known that she was up to no
good right in front of me.

                    HEDGE
That owl is a mean owl. A two-faced,
mean, owl.

                    TESS
Bark, you saw her putting eggshells
near the tree. Do you know anything
else about the owl?

                    BARK
Yes. Scowl's the name of the bird. She
sharpened her talons on my wood this
morning. Go to the Fairy Tree. You are
gonna need a magical creature for this
situation.

                    HEDGE
Bark. You're the only magical creature
Tess needs.

                    TESS
Why fairies? Tell me why I should get
advice from a fairy?

                    BARK
I knew a tree in the forest who was
taken advantage of by this human. The
tree had no tree left, was a piece of
wood until a fairy came and fixed the
tree back to life again.

                    HEDGE
How did the fairy manage to do that?

                    BARK
I don't know! They don't tell secrets
about their magic. Who knows about the
why's of their ways?

                    HEDGE
So where can Tess borrow a fairy?

                    BARK
The Fairy Express is the place to go.

                    TESS
That's where I need to go right now! I
have to get the egg back in time before
my other eggs hatch. Hedge, will you
come with me? To the Fairy Express and
to whatever comes next?

                    HEDGE
You don't even have to ask.

ACT ONE

SCENE TWO

SETTING: The Fairy Express tree

(Characters in the Scene: TESS, HEDGE, FAIRY EXPRESS EMPLOYEE, SASHA.)

                    TESS
I have never met an actual fairy. I'm
so excited!

                    HEDGE
I don't believe we need a fairy to get
your egg back.

                    TESS
We are not leaving here without a
fairy. The owl who stole my egg is not
going to get away with this. No way can
we take on that giant alone.

SCOWL'S NEST

HEDGE
Well. We've reached the fairy tree.

FAIRY EXPRESS EMPLOYEE
Fairy Express, how can I help you?

TESS
Hello. My names Tess. This is Hedge. We would like to order one fairy, preferably one who is okay with traveling at night as we are nocturnal.

FAIRY EXPRESS EMPLOYEE
And what would you need this fairy for?

TESS
We need it for a rescue mission.

FAIRY EXPRESS EMPLOYEE
Who needs to be rescued?

HEDGE
Why so many questions?

FAIRY EXPRESS EMPLOYEE
It helps us to find the right fairy for you.

TESS
My egg needs to be rescued! She was stolen by another owl two days ago. I want to find the Owl and take my egg back.

FAIRY EXPRESS EMPLOYEE
Isn't losing an egg common for most birds?

                    TESS
I'm not like most birds. My friend and
I will search every tree until we find
the owl thief's nest, fairy or no
fairy.

              FAIRY EXPRESS EMPLOYEE
Okay. Okay. Can you wait for a moment
while we choose a fairy for you?

                    HEDGE
I think he finally got the message.

     (Time goes by.)

              FAIRY EXPRESS EMPLOYEE
May I present to you, the fairy Sasha.

                    HEDGE
A pig fairy!

              FAIRY EXPRESS EMPLOYEE
How long will you need this fairy?

                    TESS
Not sure, it's tough to know when we'll
find what we're looking for.

              FAIRY EXPRESS EMPLOYEE
Two weeks then.

                    HEDGE
Are those real wings?

                    SASHA
Of course!

8

TESS
Ignore my friend Hedge. I'm grateful that you agreed to help me. We only travel at night if that's okay with you?

SASHA
No worries. I know where Scowl's nest is. Listen, we need to cross a street to get to the nest.

HEDGE
Oh no! Are you talking about Roadkill Road?

TESS
Hedge, let the fairy do his job. I need more answers about what you know about Scowl and her nest.

HEDGE
A road. Not just any road. This road has squashed so many squirrels, turtles, raccoons, and hedgehogs.

TESS
You won't be roadkill. Sasha or I can fly you across the street.

HEDGE
No way. I'm gonna cross it with my own four paws. Did my great grandfather Hedgy get a free ride across the road? No!

SCOWL'S NEST

TESS

Don't be so proud!

SASHA

Let him go. He won't change his mind.

SETTING: Roadkill Road

SASHA

Tess, I've flown across this road many times. I don't look down because of how fast the cars are going.

TESS

Hopefully, the cars don't see fairies. That would distract me if I were a car.

HEDGE

Okay. I'll see you guys on the other side of the road.

TESS

Are you sure you don't want me...?

HEDGE

No! Go.

TESS and SASHA fly across the street.

TESS

Hedge! Come on!

(HEDGE does not cross right away, he just looks across the road, closes his eyes, and shakes.)

                    SASHA
That's it. I'm gonna get him myself. No
one wants to see a flat hedgehog.

*SASHA flies across the road and grabs
HEDGE, taking him back to the other
side. HEDGE does not realize this is
happening.*

                    HEDGE
I did it!

                    TESS
Well, let's just say that someone gave
you a ride.

                    HEDGE
What?

                    SASHA
Nevermind. Let's just acknowledge that
we got across without losing a wing...

                    IIEDGE
Or my feet! Whoa, look at those cars
go.

                SQUIRREL GROUP
Hey Fairy Pig, can you get us across
the street, too?

                    TESS
Just ignore them.

SCOWL'S NEST

                    SASHA
They seem so helpless.

                    TESS
Don't even think about it. They can
wait in line at the Fairy Express like
we did.

Sasha! What should we do Hedge?

                    HEDGE
Two words, no diversions!

                    SQUIRREL GROUP
Hey. We're waiting for a lift here.

                    HEDGE
Squirrels, the fairy said no! Bye now!

ACT ONE

SCENE THREE

SETTING: Somewhere in the forest

(Characters in the Scene: SASHA, TESS, HEDGE, SCOWL, BARK, BABY ONE, BABY TWO, and BABY THREE)

> SASHA
> The only thing that has ever taken me off course like that is a nice mud bath...You both should know, that's not the first time I've said no to a mammal. Just last week, Scowl asked me to steal. She was angry that one of her eggs fell off her nest.

> TESS
> What? And you're just telling us now? Why didn't you say that before?

                    SASHA
I just wanted you to believe that I
knew what to do without a tip-off. It
would be more impressive if I figured
it out myself.

                    HEDGE
You're a fairy. Isn't that impressive
enough?

                    TESS
Tell me why you said no to Scowl but
you said yes to us?

                    SASHA
Stealing goes against fairy conduct. So
I never agreed to it.

                    HEDGE
This smells like trouble. How do we
know that he's on our side?

                    SASHA
I am with you on this. If I didn't care,
I wouldn't have helped you cross
Roadkill Road. Does that sound like a
friend or a troublemaker?

                    TESS
Okay. Thanks for the explanation. Just
be more upfront with details. No more
"just trust me I know what I'm doing."
What can we expect when we get to the
nest?

SCOWL'S NEST

SASHA

The nest is on a tree with sharp poisonous pinecones. You have to avoid them at all costs.

HEDGE

How do you know what we're up against?

SASHA

Scowl told me. It has even poisoned fairies. The tree, not the owl.

HEDGE

What are we going to do to get your egg back?

TESS

Well, since you are good at digging tunnels, why don't you...

HEDGE

Me! Why not Sasha? I thought that fairies are supposed to do the save-the -egg work?

TESS

Not one of us is going to do everything. Sasha and I will distract Scowl while you dig a tunnel to the tree.

HEDGE

So, you want me to dig a tunnel. What is the point of digging? Never thought I'd say that.

SCOWL'S NEST

SASHA

You dig the tunnel, then you climb the tree and...

TESS

Find my egg. Then roll the egg back through the tunnel.

HEDGE

How will I know which egg to pick?

SASHA

He has a point. I know! I will give you the power to know which egg it is. A mother's instincts.

TESS

Will I lose my mother owl instincts if you share it with Hedge?

SASHA

Not a chance.

HEDGE

I've never been a babysitter, let alone a mother. Okay. Yes.

SASHA

Whoa. Prey helping predator.

TESS

No. Friend helping friend.

(Time change.)

SASHA

I see the tree up ahead.

TESS
Wow. Okay, now what?

SCOWL
Sasha? What are you doing here with
her?

SASHA
I'm here to save the egg that you stole.

SCOWL
You decided to be this owl's fairy, yet
you never agreed to be mine.

TESS
Sasha will never be your fairy just
like my egg will never be yours.

SCOWL
You will never get it back.

SASHA
Scowl, you are wrong about that
prediction.

SCOWL
Fine! I'll tell you why I will win and
you will fail. I'll kill you before you
get your claws on my nest.

SASHA
You'll have to catch us first.

SCOWL
They should have turned you into pork
instead of a fairy.

SCOWL'S NEST

(SCOWL chases SASHA and TESS around the forest.)

                    HEDGE
Wow, this nest sure is impressive.
Here's the egg! Those mother's
instincts powers really pay off.

*(HEDGE'S mother instincts allow him
to tell that there are more unhatched
owl chicks in the nest that had been
stolen, too.)*

                    SCOWL
My eggs are in danger. Killing you will
have to wait.

                    SASHA
She will be coming back to a smaller
nest.

                    TESS
What do we do now?

                    SASHA
We are gonna go back to the tunnel and
wait for Hedge.

                    HEDGE
I'm back with your egg!

                    TESS
Thank goodness! We did it. And still in
one piece!

SCOWL'S NEST

                    SASHA
We're not done with this fight. We have
to destroy that owl or she'll keep
stealing eggs.

                    TESS
We can't harm that owl. It's an
endangered species.

                    HEDGE
That owl didn't only have your egg. I
noticed other eggs that were not hers.

                    SASHA
You left the others in the nest! How
could you do that? What happened to
your mother's instincts?

                    HEDGE
I'm not naturally maternal.

                    TESS
Let's go home now. I miss my nest.

                    SASHA
I have to go back to Scowl's nest
because more eggs need to be saved.

    (SCOWL appears out of nowhere. HEDGE
runs back into the tunnel.)

                    SCOWL
I'm not done with you!

    (They fly towards the highway.)

SCOWL'S NEST

SASHA
Eat fairy dust, owl!

(Fairy dust flies in SCOWL'S face. A car hits the owl and she falls to the ground.)

SCOWL
Ahh! I'm the last of my kind.

TESS
My egg broke. I must have dropped it when Scowl came charging at us.

(Talks to the broken egg.)

I messed up. I'm sorry, little egg.

SASHA
Tess I....what ever happened to Hedge?

HEDGE
Here I am.

TESS
You crossed the road by yourself!

HEDGE
Oh yeah, I did! I was so worried about my friends that I just sort of forgot the whole roadkill thing.

(HEDGE notices the broken egg.)

Your egg. Is that the egg?

                    TESS
Yes. Sasha, are you still planning on
going back for the others?

   (SASHA nods.)

                    HEDGE
You know, fairies should take breaks,
too.

                    SASHA
I'm stubborn.

                    HEDGE
Good luck with saving more eggs.

                    TESS
It's time that I go back to my woods.
I have three eggs that should be
hatching soon.

   (SASHA bows and leaves.)

SETTING: owl tree.

                    HEDGE
We haven't seen Sasha since he decided
to search for the eggs.

                    BARK
Makes sense. Fairies come and go.

   (SASHA appears.)

                    SASHA
Have you seen Tess?

SCOWL'S NEST

                        BARK
I'll let her know you're looking for
her. I can't believe I just talked to
a fairy.

                        SASHA
What have you been up too?

                        HEDGE
Sleeping. Eating. Rolling in dirt,
digging. My routine is very
predictable.

                        SASHA
Hmmm...

                        TESS
What are you doing here?

                        SASHA
After we went our separate ways, I
searched for the homes of the other
eggs. This egg still needs a guardian.

                        TESS
That's a shame. Not all eggs live to
hatch and meet their mothers.

                        SASHA
You're right. I came here because I
wanted to offer you this egg.

                        TESS
This used to be Scowl's egg, wasn't it?
I can tell.

SASHA
Yes. It was. The breed is endangered.
I want this egg to live so the species
doesn't become extinct.

TESS
And you want me to be the mom?

SASHA
Yes. If you want to be.

TESS
Let me talk it over with my owlets
first. I want them to be the final
judges. Besides, I'm kind of biased.

Oh babies?

BABY ONE, BABY TWO, BABY THREE
Yes Mama?

TESS
The fairy Sasha, the one that I told
you about, wants us to keep an egg that
lost its mother.

BABY ONE, BABY TWO, BABY THREE
It doesn't have a mother?

TESS
No. If I receive the egg from Sasha,
I'll be its new mother and you will
have another sibling.

BABY ONE, BABY TWO, BABY THREE
Will it look like us?

                    TESS
No. But it will hatch to be an owl just
like you and me. What do you say?

(BABY ONE, BABY TWO, and BABY THREE
huddle together.)

BABY ONE, BABY TWO, BABY THREE
We say yes!

                    TESS
I'm so glad that yes is your answer.

    Setting: Below the treetop.

                    BARK
I hear a lot of chirping up there.

                    HEDGE
Hey Sasha, Tess is back.

                    SASHA
Thank you for giving this egg another
life.

                    HEDGE
Another life?

                    TESS
Well, thank you for bringing him to me.

    (SASHA bows.)

SCOWL'S NEST

>   HEDGE
> Where are you going?

>   SASHA
> Back to the Fairy Tree. Happy to say
> that I didn't leave with a nest half
> empty.

> *(SASHA leaves the scene.)*

> *(The next evening.)*

>   HEDGE
> I can't believe that you adopted this
> egg. This owl's mom is the reason why
> your egg died!

>   TESS
> You probably think that when the bird
> grows up he will try to run away.

>   HEDGE
> Running away will be the most harmless
> thing that it can do to you.

>   TESS
> You have no idea what this owl is going
> to be like.

>   HEDGE
> If I were you, I would leave it in the
> woods and let nature take its course.
> According to Bark, the nature of
> Spotted Owls is that they are more
> aggressive than other owls--aggressive
> and endangered.

SCOWL'S NEST

TESS
You cannot predict the nature of an owl
that hasn't been born yet. Our
friendship is the opposite of how
nature should be, Hedge. I'm supposed
to eat you but I can't because I'm a
picky eater Predator.

HEDGE
Please don't do this. I don't want him
to hurt you. Bark and I can't stop him
from trying.

TESS
This egg was meant for me. And I'll be
the only mother, so stop squeaking and
get used to it.

HEDGE
Fine. Don't listen. I'm going to…leave.

(TESS talks to the egg.)

TESS
If I look into the shell of this unborn
baby and only see Scowl, then I will
have to look past it.

(Time goes by. BARK sees TESS flying
back with something in her talons.)

BARK
You brought a nest back? Here?

SCOWL'S NEST

TESS

Scowl's nest. I want my egg to feel more at home.

HEDGE

When your owlets leave the nest, they may decide that hedgehogs are their favorite food on the menu.

TESS

Come on, how do you know? I'll train them to dislike the taste of hedge hogs.

HEDGE

What's the plan, Tess?

TESS

I haven't come up with a plan yet.

HEDGE

Well, you have a while to figure it out because hibernation starts next week. Maybe I should snag a bird's nest to hide in.

THE END

Acknowledgments

I would like to thank the
following people for helping me
bring this play to fruition: my
parents Gary and Debra Hudes, Sara
Bruya, M.K. Williams, Ed Hanna,
and Bobby Zislis.

ABOUT THE AUTHOR

Jennifer Hudes was a first prize winner of the Philadelphia Young Playwrights New Voices Workshop. She earned her Bachelor Of Arts degree in English from Temple University, where she studied theatre and literature. Hudes lives with her family in Pennsylvania.